JL

he Sewer Sleuth

Stories linking with the History
National Curriculum Key Stage 2.

First published in 1997 by Franklin Watts

This paperback edition published in 1998

Franklin Watts
96 Leonard Street
London EC2A 4RH

Franklin Watts Australia
14 Mars Road
Lane Cove
NSW 2006

The right of Julia Jarman tc
the Author of this Work has
her in accordance with the (
and Patents Act, 1988.

Editor: Suzy Jenvey
Series editor: Paula Borton
Designer: Kirstie Billinghar
Consultant: Dr Anne Milla

A CIP catalogue record for ι
is available from the British Library.

ISBN   0 7496 3128 7 (pbk)
       0 7496 2590 2 (hbk)

Dewey Classification 941.081

Printed in Great Britain

The Sewer Sleuth

by
Julia Jarman
Illustrations by Liz Minichiello

W
FRANKLIN WATTS
NEW YORK • LONDON • SYDNEY

1

A Bad Sign

Sounding more cheerful than he felt, Tom said, "Sarah, I'll try not to be long. I'll be as fast as a ferret, you'll see!"

As he edged open the door, sunlight showed up his sister's blue skin. It was a bad sign. She needed water – *quickly.*

He peered out. Good - no one about.
It wouldn't do to let anyone know they
were on their own at home. Home?
Somehow it didn't seem the right word,
although it had been once.

In the corner of the cellar room they
lived in, his sister was sleeping on a heap
of straw. There'd been a bed and chairs
once, but they had gone months ago.
They had been sold to pay the rent and
buy food.

As Tom started off along the narrow street, dark, grimy house walls rose up on either side, casting him in shadow. He tried to hurry, but he didn't feel too good himself. If only the pump wasn't so far away, or if it wasn't so hot - or if he wasn't so hungry.

As he made his way up Broad Street, Tom noticed how empty it was. Usually it was ever so busy - now fear of cholera was keeping people away. Was that what he could smell? It was in the air, people said.

As Tom came into the alley the smell grew stronger. Turning his head to watch the dead-cart coming down the street with its load of dead bodies, he nearly slipped.

Ugh! The public privy was overflowing again. That's what the smell was.

The flies rose from the filth at his feet as he picked his way carefully along. The alley hummed with their sound. Why did they say people were dying like flies? The glistening black creatures were full of life. Not like...Tom tried not to think about the bluey-grey bodies of his mum and dad and

three little brothers. He must think of the living now, and get back to Sarah. If she didn't get a drink soon...

But it wasn't his lucky day. There was someone at the pump. Tom hung back.

Definitely not his lucky day. When his turn came, the water dripped out in a thin brown trickle, and it took him ages to fill the cup.

And when he did get back to the cellar, there was a man in a top hat waiting for him.

"Tom Cracknell?"

Too weary to run, he couldn't stop the man taking hold of his shoulder.

"Are you Tom Cracknell?" The man's  voice was kind as he looked down from beneath bushy eyebrows, but Tom was suspicious.

He'd heard of these types. Toffs. One minute they were talking kindly. Next minute they had you in the workhouse.

"I'm Doctor Snow," the man went on. "Your sister needs help, Tom. She's very ill."

So he'd found Sarah. That changed things.

"I'd like to take her home. With proper care she may recover. You can come too," he added. "Some people do survive the cholera, you know."

Proper care for Sarah? That was an offer he couldn't turn down.

But as Tom followed the doctor who carried Sarah to the gig waiting by the roadside, he was still suspicious.

2

Another World

Doctor Snow's house was like another world, not just a different part of London. There was a garden at the front and at the back, and the rooms inside were enormous.

But on that first day Tom only saw part of it. When they arrived, a servant girl

opened the front door.

Sweeping past her, Doctor Snow said, "Dora, tell your mistress I have a patient."

For a moment Tom thought she was going to close the door in his face. But a large lady appeared and told her to give Tom something to eat.

With a "certainly, Mrs Snow", the red-haired Dora led the way to the kitchen.

But when she put a glass of milk in front of him, it seemed to float above the table.

"It's to drink, idiot," he heard Dora say.

But now he felt as if he was going to be sick. He felt a terrible pain in his stomach.

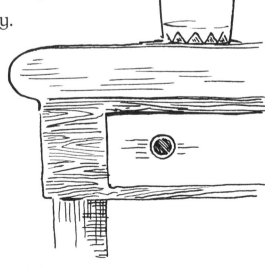

Doubling up, he heard Dora say, "Oh my gawd, you've got it too. Mrs Snow!"

Then everything went black.

◆

When he next opened his eyes, everything was bright and shiny. So he thought he'd died and gone to Heaven! There was an angel by his side, he was sure there was.

"Come back to the land of the living, 'ave we?" said the angel with a cockney accent.

Did angels have freckles and red hair?

"Mrs Snow, Tom's back with us!" yelled Dora.

Mrs Snow appeared. Tom smiled up into her friendly face, but he felt too weak to say anything.

Helped by Dora and Mrs Snow, he drank a few sips of clean water, then slept again. As he drifted in and out of sleep, strange smells floated around him.

Honeysuckle – wafted in by the clean muslin curtains.

Turpentine - from the hot flannels Mrs
Smith applied to his aching stomach.

Beef tea - from the kitchen.

Mrs Snow sponged his hot body and
rubbed his cramped limbs. Tom began to
feel his strength returning, and his mind
became full of thoughts of Sarah.

Was she alive? He hardly dared ask. But she had survived too!

Mrs Snow, seeing his worried face, sat by Tom's bed and told him the good news. She said that they had both been very ill for days - Sarah worse than Tom. But Dr Snow had treated many cholera patients, and with his care they had both pulled through.

She took Tom - in a bath chair – to see Sarah.

"You're the lucky ones," Dora said when she brought them lunch one day. "There's not many folks as'd share their homes with the likes of you."

Now the brother and sister were in the same room, their beds side by side, eating meaty broth from china dishes with silver spoons.

Dora smoothed the creases out of their white bedsheets.

"The doctor's used to grander cases than this," she said. "He's even treated Queen Victoria!"

"How will we ever thank him?" said Sarah, who still hardly had the strength to eat.

"You could help me solve the Mystery of Broad Street," said a deep voice.

It was Doctor Snow himself, standing in the doorway.

3

A Mass Murderer

Tom wasn't sure he'd heard right.

"I'm a sort of investigator," the doctor said, and Tom perked up.

He *had* heard right! The doctor was a detective!

"And I need your assistance," he went on.

"I'm trying to find the cause of cholera, you see."

Tom couldn't hide his disappointment. He thought the doctor had meant a proper mystery – a robbery or a murder.

Doctor Snow seemed to read his mind. Sitting down, he said gently, "Cholera has killed millions of people this year, Tom, some of them close to you. Doesn't that make it a sort of murderer? A mass murderer, even?"

Tom thought of the family he used to have being carried away in the dead-cart.

"Wouldn't finding the cause of cholera be like arresting that murderer?" the doctor said.

Tom had to agree, but he secretly wondered if the doctor was stupid.

Bad air caused cholera, everyone said so - except Freddy Snoddy who said it was the water. But that was only an excuse to drink beer all the time! Freddy was a drunk!

Again the doctor seemed to read his mind.

"If it's bad air," he said, "why do people on only one side of Broad Street seem to get it? Have you noticed that, Tom?"

"Yes," Tom replied. He remembered his mam saying sadly, "It's a curse. Our side's cursed."

"But everyone breathes the same air, no matter which side of the street they live on! Yes?" asked Doctor Snow.

"Yes," said Tom, but he still wasn't sure what the doctor was getting at.

"Well - don't you see? That proves the disease isn't carried in the air! Otherwise everyone would catch it - not just people on one side. So *something else* causes cholera - something on one side of the street only!"

"And you want me to help you find it?" said Tom.

"I *need* you to help me," the doctor said.

"Help me find the difference between one side of the street and the other, and you'll have helped find the cause of cholera!"

The doctor had been trying on his own, he said, but people wouldn't answer his questions, wouldn't even open their doors sometimes.

"It's 'cos you're a toff," said Tom.
"Toffs is bad news in Broad Street. Toffs
mean busybodies, bailiffs, debt collectors..."

"Exactly. So I need your help to gather
clues, Tom." Now the doctor's big black
boots thumped the floorboards as he
paced the room.

"We've got to ask people lots of questions."

"Tom'd be good at that," said Sarah. "He's got the gift of the gab, Mam always said."

"Can Sarah come too?" Tom asked.

Doctor Snow shook his head.

"She's not well enough yet. But you soon will be. Now, how about it?"

A detective's assistant! Tom liked the idea.

"When can we start?" he said.

4

Detective Tom

But when Tom stood in Broad Street again, a few days later, he didn't feel so keen. Just the stench brought back bad memories - of himself in rags, for one thing.

Now he wore breeches and a smart woollen jacket - not too smart, he hoped.

He wanted the neighbours to recognize him, after all - but he couldn't help trying to keep his new boots clean as he followed Doctor Snow up the street.

The doctor was stomping along - he didn't seem to notice the mud splashing around his feet.

"Ready, Tom? Remember what we're here for?" he said when at last he stopped, about halfway along, near The Grapes public house.

"We're looking for differences between one side of the street and the other. Those differences are our clues. Put them all together and we'll find our murderer!"

He took a notebook from his pocket. Tom knew there were lists of questions in that notebook. He'd helped the doctor make them.

"Let's begin spotting the difference, Tom!"

Both sides of the street looked almost identical, that was the trouble. The tiny back-to-back houses on both sides looked exactly the same,

though the street was busier since he'd last been there.

Now that the weather was cooler, the cholera epidemic had subsided a bit, so people were venturing in to the street again.

But Tom knew too well what the insides of those houses were like - all crammed with people, a family to each room.

None of them had water taps, or water closets like the doctor's house had. So it was really hard to keep clean. And open fires - the only place to cook - filled the rooms with soot and smoke.

Not to mention rats and mice and cockroaches...

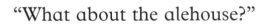

"What about the alehouse?"

Tom was glad when the doctor interrupted his dreary thoughts. The Grapes, on the right hand side, was one obvious difference.

But Tom had to disappoint the doctor who looked hopeful. *Everyone* went to The Grapes, he said, whichever side they lived on - when they had the money.

And some when they didn't - Freddy Snoddy
for instance - so The Grapes wasn't a clue.

But Freddy Snoddy was, it seemed!
Doctor Snow was very interested in Fred
who was sitting on the
steps of the
alehouse, his big
red nose shining.

He seemed pleased to see Tom, and Tom introduced him to the doctor. At first Mr Snoddy was suspicious, but Tom managed to reassure him that the doctor was a *really good cove!*

"Mr Snoddy, have you ever had the cholera?" asked Doctor Snow.

"Never..sh! Never..s! Never..sh!"

"And why is that, Mr Snoddy?"

Doctor Snow couldn't understand Mr Snoddy's reply, but Tom could! Mr Snoddy thought the government was poisoning the water – to get rid of poor people - so he never drank it.

To Tom's surprise the doctor made a note of his drunken replies, labelling them CLUE NUMBER ONE.

Then he said, "Right, Tom. Let's see what else we can find!"

The plan was to go to every house in the street. But first they went to the room in the cellar where Tom and Sarah had lived, because Tom had had an idea.

He'd told the doctor about a black mould
which grew there.

Tom led the way down the steps,
holding the lantern.

How could they have lived there?

In a corner was the straw
he and Sarah had slept on.

The doctor removed a piece of brick covered with the black mould. It was all over the cellar - walls, ceiling, and floor. It was slimy and smelled horribly musty. Could that cause the cholera?

"Maybe the air *inside* the houses causes the disease," Tom suggested. "Not the air in the street?"

"You could be on to something," said Doctor Snow. He tucked the piece of brick carefully in his pocket and wrote in his notebook:

CLUE NUMBER 2.

5

In Search of Clues

Now the two detectives left the cellar and crossed to a house opposite. Tom banged the knocker, but it was a while before anyone answered.

Then Mrs Tanner opened the door but was about to shut it again until she saw

Tom, who persuaded her to let them in.

The same musty smell hit them almost immediately despite the smell of potatoes boiling on the fire. And they soon found some of the same black mould in the corner of the room.

"So the mould is eliminated," said the doctor.

Tom wished the doctor didn't use such big words.

"Eliminated, dear boy! No longer a clue. This is the healthy side of the street. There's mould here - and there was mould on the other side. So it can't be the mould."

But Doctor Snow wasn't finished. He started on a list of questions - about food.

Mrs Tanner wasn't too pleased about that.

"We eat taters and bread mostly," she said.

"And?" prompted Doctor Snow.

"Sometimes, as a special treat, we 'as bread and taters," she answered sarcastically.

"And where do you get them, Mrs Tanner?" Doctor Snow was polite and patient.

"Bakers in Victoria Street. Market off Victoria Street."

"And what do you cook the potatoes in?"

"Water, of course."

"And where do you get your water from?"

"The pump."

"And where do you work?" he said.

"You're the clever one," she answered.

"Use your eyes!"

Tom couldn't help grinning. All around the room there were shirts bristling with pins. It was obvious that Mrs Tanner worked at home, sewing for one of the Bond Street tailors.

Out on the street the doctor added
more clues to the list:

3. BREAD, 4. POTATOES.

But he crossed them out again when
they'd interviewed Mrs Greco on the other
side of the road, and discovered that her
family lived on bread and potatoes too.

All morning they criss-crossed from one side of the street to the other, asking the same questions. Some people were polite, some were rude, but they all gave similar answers.

They ate similar food.

They had similar jobs - if they had jobs at all - in the clothing trade, as seamstresses making clothes for the shops in Bond Street and Regent Street, or as labourers for builders.

A few were costermongers with barrows who went around selling fruit and vegetables.

It was nearly lunchtime when they thought they'd found an important clue. Mrs Casey, who always had tea on the go, offered them a cup. When Doctor Snow declined, she said, "You won't catch no cholera here," and pointed to the branches of elderberry hanging at the window. "None of us 'ave 'ad it."

It seemed that that was true. Most of her large family were in the room with her.

Could it really be the elderberry that kept the disease away?

Doctor Snow made a note of it, but when they went next door, a woman pointed to a body in the corner of the room.

Her husband had just died of cholera, she said, despite taking Mrs Casey's advice.

Tom and Doctor Snow both noted the elderberry in the window.

It was a sad end to the morning. Tom felt a failure. Being a detective wasn't exciting - it was just hard work.

Doctor Snow said, "You were a big help, Tom. They wouldn't have talked to me if you hadn't been there."

But that didn't make him feel any better.

6

Solving the Mystery

Dora was serving up lunch when they got back to the house, and sniffed when the doctor asked her to lay a place for Tom. She thought he should eat in the kitchen.

Mrs Snow urged them all to eat up. There was lovely roast mutton with

potatoes, parsnips and gravy and fresh peas
and mint sauce, but Tom didn't feel like
eating. He couldn't help thinking of Mrs
Tanner's little pot of potatoes.

Doctor Snow wasn't eating much either.

"I can't understand it," he said,
pushing peas around his plate with a fork.
"Those people in Broad Street. They
breathe the same air, they eat the same

food from the same shops. They do similar sorts of jobs. They drink the same water, drawn from the same pump..."

"No they don't," said Tom.

"Don't what?" said the doctor.

"Use the same pump."

"*What?*" Doctor Snow's bushy eyebrows jumped and he dropped his fork on his plate.

Tom realized that he was about to say something very important.

"There are two pumps. *Our* side uses the Broad Street pump. The other side uses the one in Court Street. It's nearer for them, see."

Doctor Snow leaped out of his seat.

"Two different pumps! That must be it! That must be the answer!"

He thumped the table with excitement. Mrs Snow threw her arms around Tom. Dora, coming in to clear the dishes, gave him a filthy look but Tom didn't care.

He wasn't sure how - but he'd just helped solve the mystery of Broad Street!

"Come on, Tom! Show me!" said Doctor Snow.

"We must tell Sarah," said Tom. She was still resting in bed.

A few minutes later they were racing back

to Broad Street in Doctor Snow's gig.

Then they were getting out by the stinking alley.

"Mind, sir - it's slippery," warned Tom.

There was the overflowing privy at the end. There was the pump.

Doctor Snow pointed to the dirty brown sludge on the pavement.

"You see, Tom? That *sewage* is seeping from the privy into the water supply."

Grabbing hold of the wooden pump handle, Doctor Snow broke it off with a satisfying crack.

"Now no one can use it," he said.

Next, Tom and Dr Snow visited the pump on Court Street.

"It's cleaner here," said Tom.

Dr Snow nodded. "Both sides of the street will use this pump for their water now," he said. "Let's see if that stops the cholera!"

It did! There were no more cases of cholera in Broad Street that summer.

Doctor Snow wrote a report for the government and Queen Victoria herself, explaining that the cholera germ lived in dirty water.

Looking back it all seemed so obvious.

Mr Snoddy was right. So was Mrs Casey. Ale and tea were made with boiled water and boiling helped kill the germs. So in hot weather, when people drank more cold water, there was more cholera.

One clue led to another - but they all led back to the pump in Broad Street.

Notes

Housing and Health in Victorian Times

This story is set in London in 1854, when thousands of people had poured into the city to find work in the new factories. Lots of houses were being built, but wages were low. Often families could only afford to rent one room, so overcrowding was common.

Houses

Houses didn't have the facilities that we expect today. They were often terraced (joined together in a row), and back to back too. So there were no gardens or even back yards. They had very few windows so they were dark and badly ventilated.

Inside, only the rich had running water and water closets (toilets). Water for washing and drinking came from a pump. The pump was usually in the street or in a yard at the end of the block. Several large families would use one pump.

Poor families also had to share an outside privy (toilet). You sat on a wooden seat and the waste collected beneath or drained into the soil. It wasn't flushed away.

Sometimes the privies were emptied by the night soil man. Then the sewage (waste from the privies) was tipped into the River Thames. The water companies pumped the dirty water out, purified it as well as they could, and piped it back in to the pumps of the poor and the taps of the rich.

People didn't know about invisible bacteria until the end of the century. They thought that water was clean if it looked clean. Looking back, it doesn't surprise us that disease was common and killed thousands of people in frequent epidemics. The most common diseases were typhoid, tuberculosis and cholera.

Cholera

This was a horrific disease. The symptoms were violent stomach pains, vomiting, diarrhoea and convulsions. The victim's skin turned blue and breathing became difficult.

Half those who caught it died, usually very quickly. To add to the horror of the disease the victims would sometimes go on convulsing – having violent fits - after death. It was often thought of as a tyrannical king - King Cholera - or a deadly ghost haunting the cities.

Epidemics of cholera struck Britain in 1831-2, 1848-9, 1853-4, 1865-6, and 1893. It was particularly common in poor areas, where people died in their thousands. In 1832, 18,000 people died. In 1854, 20,000 people died. After 1855, there were fewer cases and fewer deaths.

Hospitals

There were hospitals - quite famous ones, like St Thomas's - but people avoided them. They were thought of as places where you died, not where you were cured.

They were often rough and dirty places. Florence Nightingale hadn't yet begun her reform of the nursing profession in Great Britain, though she was putting her ideas into practice in the Crimean War (1854-6).

Doctor John Snow

He really lived! He was Queen Victoria's doctor and he did discover the cause of cholera. He suspected that poor living conditions caused the disease and he set out to prove it. He was one of several reformers who campaigned for improvements in the housing conditions of the poor, and in factory conditions.

There is a pub named after him in Broad Street, now called Broadwick Street, in London.